5 BEST
SHORT STORIES
— VOL 1 —

RABINDRANATH TAGORE

One of the leading figures of Bengali literature, **Rabindranath Tagore** was born on May 7, 1861. He was brought up in a literary, intellectual, and social household, and began writing at an early age. The bibliography of his writing contains more than two hundred works and around two thousand two hundred songs. From poetic dramas, social plays, short stories, philosophical and critical essays, and travelogues to letters, memoirs, lyrics, drawings, and paintings, Tagores life was marked by uninterrupted literary and artistic creations. Many of Tagores stories and novels have been adapted for film and television. His works continue to be translated into many languages worldwide.

CONTENTS

I

THE KABULIWALAH

My five years' old daughter Mini cannot live without chattering. I really believe that in all her life she has not wasted a minute in silence. Her mother is often vexed at this, and would stop her prattle, but I would not. To see Mini quiet is unnatural, and I cannot bear it long. And so my own talk with her is always lively.

One morning, for instance, when I was in the midst of the seventeenth chapter of my new novel, my little Mini stole into the room, and putting her hand into mine, said: "Father! Ramdayal the door-keeper calls a crow a krow! He doesn't know anything, does he?"

Before I could explain to her the differences of language in this world, she was embarked on the full tide of another subject. "What do you think, Father? Bhola says there is an elephant in the clouds, blowing water out of his trunk, and that is why it rains!"

And then, darting off anew, while I sat still making ready some reply to this last saying: "Father! what relation is Mother to you?"

With a grave face I contrived to say: "Go and play with Bhola, Mini! I am busy!"

The window of my room overlooks the road. The child had seated herself at my feet near my table, and was playing softly, drumming on her knees. I was hard at work on my seventeenth chapter, where Pratap Singh, the hero, had just caught Kanchanlata, the heroine, in his arms, and was about to escape with her by the third-story window of the castle, when all of a sudden Mini left her play, and ran to the window, crying: "A Kabuliwalah! a Kabuliwalah!" Sure enough in the street below was a Kabuliwalah, passing slowly along. He wore the loose, soiled clothing of his people, with a tall turban; there was a bag on his back, and he carried boxes of grapes in his hand.

I cannot tell what were my daughter's feelings at the sight of this man, but she began to call him loudly. "Ah!" I thought, "he will come in, and my seventeenth chapter will never be finished!" At which exact moment the Kabuliwalah turned, and looked up at the child. When she saw this, overcome by terror, she fled to her mother's protection and disappeared. She had a blind belief that inside the bag, which the big man carried, there were perhaps two or three other children like herself. The pedlar meanwhile entered my doorway and greeted me with a smiling face.

So precarious was the position of my hero and my heroine, that my first impulse was to stop and buy something, since the man had been called. I made some small purchases, and a conversation began about Abdurrahman, the Russians, the English, and the Frontier Policy.

As he was about to leave, he asked: "And where is the little girl, sir?"

And I, thinking that Mini must get rid of her false fear, had her brought out.

She stood by my chair, and looked at the Kabuliwalah and his bag. He offered her nuts and raisins, but she would not be tempted, and only clung the closer to me, with all her doubts increased.

This was their first meeting.

One morning, however, not many days later, as I was leaving the house, I was startled to find Mini, seated on a bench near the door, laughing and talking, with the great Kabuliwalah at her feet. In all her life, it appeared, my small daughter had never found so patient a listener, save her father. And already the corner of her little *sari* was stuffed with almonds and raisins, the gift of her visitor. "Why did you give her those?" I said, and taking out an eight-anna bit, I handed it to him. The man accepted the money without demur, and slipped it into his pocket.

Alas, on my return an hour later, I found the unfortunate coin had made twice its own worth of trouble! For the Kabuliwalah had given it to Mini; and her mother, catching sight of the bright round object, had pounced on the child with: "Where did you get that eight-anna bit?"

"The Kabuliwalah gave it me," said Mini cheerfully.

"The Kabuliwalah gave it you!" cried her mother much shocked. "O Mini! how could you take it from him?"

I, entering at the moment, saved her from impending disaster, and proceeded to make my own inquiries.

It was not the first or second time, I found, that the two had met. The Kabuliwalah had overcome the child's first terror by a judicious bribery of nuts and almonds, and the two were now great friends.

They had many quaint jokes, which afforded them much amusement. Seated in front of him, looking down on his gigantic frame in all her tiny dignity, Mini would ripple her face with laughter and begin: "O Kabuliwalah! Kabuliwalah!

what have you got in your bag?"

And he would reply, in the nasal accents of the mountaineer: "An elephant!" Not much cause for merriment, perhaps; but how they both enjoyed the fun! And for me, this child's talk with a grown-up man had always in it something strangely fascinating.

Then the Kabuliwalah, not to be behindhand, would take his turn: "Well, little one, and when are you going to the father-in-law's house?"

Now most small Bengali maidens have heard long ago about the father-in-law's house; but we, being a little new-fangled, had kept these things from our child, and Mini at this question must have been a trifle bewildered. But she would not show it, and with ready tact replied: "Are *you* going there?"

Amongst men of the Kabuliwalah's class, however, it is well known that the words *father-in-law's house* have a double meaning. It is a euphemism for *jail*, the place where we are well cared for, at no expense to ourselves. In this sense would the sturdy pedlar take my daughter's question. "Ah," he would say, shaking his fist at an invisible policeman, "I will thrash my father-in-law!" Hearing this, and picturing the poor discomfited relative, Mini would go off into peals of laughter, in which her formidable friend would join.

These were autumn mornings, the very time of year when kings of old went forth to conquest; and I, never stirring from my little corner in Calcutta, would let my mind wander over the whole world. At the very name of another country, my heart would go out to it, and at the sight of a foreigner in the streets, I would fall to weaving a network of dreams,—the mountains, the glens, and the forests of his distant home, with his cottage in its setting, and the free and independent life of far-away wilds. Perhaps the scenes of travel conjure themselves up before me and pass and repass in my imagination all the more vividly, because I lead such a vegetable existence that a call to travel would fall upon me like a thunder-bolt. In the presence of this Kabuliwalah I was immediately transported to the foot of arid mountain peaks, with narrow little defiles twisting in and out amongst their towering heights. I could see the string of camels bearing the merchandise, and the company of turbanned merchants carrying some their queer old firearms, and some their spears, journeying downward towards the plains. I could see—. But at some such point Mini's mother would intervene, imploring me to "beware of that man."

Mini's mother is unfortunately a very timid lady. Whenever she hears a noise in the street, or sees people coming towards the house, she always jumps to the conclusion that they are either thieves, or drunkards, or snakes, or tigers, or malaria, or cockroaches, or caterpillars. Even after all these years of experience, she is not able to overcome her terror. So she was full of doubts about the Kabuliwalah, and used to beg me to keep a watchful eye on him.

I tried to laugh her fear gently away, but then she would turn round on me seriously, and ask me solemn questions:—

Were children never kidnapped?

Was it, then, not true that there was slavery in Cabul?

Was it so very absurd that this big man should be able to carry off a tiny child?

I urged that, though not impossible, it was highly improbable. But this was not enough, and her dread persisted. As it was indefinite, however, it did not seem right to forbid the man the house, and the intimacy went on unchecked.

Once a year in the middle of January Rahmun, the Kabuliwalah, was in the habit of returning to his country, and as the time approached he would be very busy, going from house to house collecting his debts. This year, however, he could always find time to come and see Mini. It would have seemed to an outsider that there was some conspiracy between the two, for when he could not come in the morning, he would appear in the evening.

Even to me it was a little startling now and then, in the corner of a dark room, suddenly to surprise this tall, loose-garmented, much bebagged man; but when Mini would run in smiling, with her "O Kabuliwalah! Kabuliwalah!" and the two friends, so far apart in age, would subside into their old laughter and their old jokes, I felt reassured.

One morning, a few days before he had made up his mind to go, I was correcting my proof sheets in my study. It was chilly weather. Through the window the rays of the sun touched my feet, and the slight warmth was very welcome. It was almost eight o'clock, and the early pedestrians were returning home with their heads covered. All at once I heard an uproar in the street, and, looking out, saw Rahmun being led away bound between two policemen, and behind them a crowd of curious boys. There were blood-stains on the clothes of the Kabuliwalah, and one of the policemen carried a knife. Hurrying out, I stopped them, and inquired what it all meant. Partly from one, partly from another, I gathered that a certain neighbour had owed the pedlar something for a Rampuri shawl, but had falsely denied having bought it, and that in the course of the quarrel Rahmun had struck him. Now, in the heat of his excitement, the prisoner began calling his enemy all sorts of names, when suddenly in a verandah of my house appeared my little Mini, with her usual exclamation: "O Kabuliwalah! Kabuliwalah!" Rahmun's face lighted up as he turned to her. He had no bag under his arm to-day, so she could not discuss the elephant with him. She at once therefore proceeded to the next question: "Are you going to the father-in-law's house?" Rahmun laughed and said: "Just where I am going, little one!" Then, seeing that the reply did not amuse the child, he held up his fettered hands. "Ah!" he said, "I would have thrashed that old father-in-law, but my hands are bound!"

On a charge of murderous assault, Rahmun was sentenced to some years' imprisonment.

Time passed away and he was not remembered. The accustomed work in the accustomed place was ours, and the thought of the once free mountaineer spending his years in prison seldom or never occurred to us. Even my light-hearted Mini, I am ashamed to say, forgot her old friend. New companions filled her life. As she grew older, she spent more of her time with girls. So much time indeed did she spend with them that she came no more, as she used to do, to her father's room. I was scarcely on speaking terms with her.

Years had passed away. It was once more autumn and we had made arrangements for our Mini's marriage. It was to take place during the Puja Holidays. With Durga returning to Kailas, the light of our home also was to depart to her husband's house, and leave her father's in the shadow.

The morning was bright. After the rains, there was a sense of ablution in the air, and the sun-rays looked like pure gold. So bright were they, that they gave a beautiful radiance even to the sordid brick walls of our Calcutta lanes. Since early dawn that day the wedding-pipes had been sounding, and at each beat my own heart throbbed. The wail of the tune, Bhairavi, seemed to intensify my pain at the approaching separation. My Mini was to be married that night.

From early morning noise and bustle had pervaded the house. In the courtyard the canopy had to be slung on its bamboo poles; the chandeliers with their tinkling sound must be hung in each room and verandah. There was no end of hurry and excitement. I was sitting in my study, looking through the accounts, when some one entered, saluting respectfully, and stood before me. It was Rahmun the Kabuliwalah. At first I did not recognise him. He had no bag, nor the long hair, nor the same vigour that he used to have. But he smiled, and I knew him again.

"When did you come, Rahmun?" I asked him.

"Last evening," he said, "I was released from jail."

The words struck harsh upon my ears. I had never before talked with one who had wounded his fellow, and my heart shrank within itself when I realised this; for I felt that the day would have been better-omened had he not turned up.

"There are ceremonies going on," I said, "and I am busy. Could you perhaps come another day?"

At once he turned to go; but as he reached the door he hesitated, and said: "May I not see the little one, sir, for a moment?" It was his belief that Mini was still the same. He had pictured her running to him as she used, calling "O Kabuliwalah! Kabuliwalah!" He had imagined too that they would laugh and talk together, just as of old. In fact, in memory of former days he had brought, carefully wrapped up in paper, a few almonds and raisins and grapes, obtained somehow from a countryman; for his own little fund was dispersed.

I said again: "There is a ceremony in the house, and you will not be able to see any one to-day."

The man's face fell. He looked wistfully at me for a moment, then said "Good morning," and went out.

I felt a little sorry, and would have called him back, but I found he was returning of his own accord. He came close up to me holding out his offerings with the words: "I brought these few things, sir, for the little one. Will you give them to her?"

I took them and was going to pay him, but he caught my hand and said: "You are very kind, sir! Keep me in your recollection. Do not offer me money!—You have a little girl: I too have one like her in my own home. I think of her, and bring fruits to your child—not to make a profit for myself."

Saying this, he put his hand inside his big loose robe, and brought out a small and dirty piece of paper. With great care he unfolded this, and smoothed it out with both hands on my table. It bore the impression of a little hand. Not a photograph. Not a drawing. The impression of an ink-smeared hand laid flat on the paper. This touch of his own little daughter had been always on his heart, as he had come year after year to Calcutta to sell his wares in the streets.

Tears came to my eyes. I forgot that he was a poor Cabuli fruit-seller, while I was—. But no, what was I more than he? He also was a father.

That impression of the hand of his little *Pārbati* in her distant mountain home reminded me of my own little Mini.

I sent for Mini immediately from the inner apartment. Many difficulties were raised, but I would not listen. Clad in the red silk of her wedding-day, with the sandal paste on her forehead, and adorned as a young bride, Mini came, and stood bashfully before me.

The Kabuliwalah looked a little staggered at the apparition. He could not revive their old friendship. At last he smiled and said: "Little one, are you going to your father-in-law's house?"

But Mini now understood the meaning of the word "father-in-law," and she could not reply to him as of old. She flushed up at the question, and stood before him with her bride-like face turned down.

I remembered the day when the Kabuliwalah and my Mini had first met, and I felt sad. When she had gone, Rahmun heaved a deep sigh, and sat down on the floor. The idea had suddenly come to him that his daughter too must have grown in this long time, and that he would have to make friends with her anew. Assuredly he would not find her as he used to know her. And besides, what might not have happened to her in these eight years?

The marriage-pipes sounded, and the mild autumn sun streamed round us. But Rahmun sat in the little Calcutta lane, and saw before him the barrenmountains of

Afghanistan.

I took out a bank-note and gave it to him, saying: "Go back to your own daughter, Rahmun, in your own country, and may the happiness of your meeting bring good fortune to my child!"

Having made this present, I had to curtail some of the festivities. I could not have the electric lights I had intended, nor the military band, and the ladies of the house were despondent at it. But to me the wedding-feast was all the brighter for the thought that in a distant land a long-lost father met again with his only child.

II

THE HOME-COMING

Phatik Chakravorti was ringleader among the boys of the village. A new mischief got into his head. There was a heavy log lying on the mud-flat of the river waiting to be shaped into a mast for a boat. He decided that they should all work together to shift the log by main force from its place and roll it away. The owner of the log would be angry and surprised, and they would all enjoy the fun. Every one seconded the proposal, and it was carried unanimously.

But just as the fun was about to begin, Mākhan, Phatik's younger brother, sauntered up and sat down on the log in front of them all without a word. The boys were puzzled for a moment. He was pushed, rather timidly, by one of the boys and told to get up; but he remained quite unconcerned. He appeared like a young philosopher meditating on the futility of games. Phatik was furious. "Mākhan," he cried, "if you don't get down this minute I'll thrash you!"

Mākhan only moved to a more comfortable position.

Now, if Phatik was to keep his regal dignity before the public, it was clear he ought to carry out his threat. But his courage failed him at the crisis. His fertile brain, however, rapidly seized upon a new manœuvre which would discomfit his brother and afford his followers an added amusement. He gave the word of command to roll the log and Mākhan over together. Mākhan heard the order and made it a point of honour to stick on. But he overlooked the fact, like those who attempt earthly fame in other matters, that there was peril in it.

The boys began to heave at the log with all their might, calling out, "One, two, three, go!" At the word "go" the log went; and with it went Mākhan's philosophy, glory and all.

The other boys shouted themselves hoarse with delight. But Phatik was a little frightened. He knew what was coming. And, sure enough, Mākhan rose from Mother Earth blind as Fate and screaming like the Furies. He rushed at Phatik and scratched his face and beat him and kicked him, and then went crying home. The first act of the drama was over.

Phatik wiped his face, and sat down on the edge of a sunken barge by the river bank, and began to chew a piece of grass. A boat came up to the landing and a middle-aged man, with grey hair and dark moustache, stepped on shore. He saw the boy sitting there doing nothing and asked him where the Chakravortis lived. Phatik went on chewing the grass and said: "Over there," but it was quite impossible to tell where he pointed. The stranger asked him again. He swung his legs to and fro on the side of the barge and said: "Go and find out," and continued to chew the grass as before.

But now a servant came down from the house and told Phatik his mother wanted him. Phatik refused to move. But the servant was the master on this occasion. He took Phatik up roughly and carried him, kicking and struggling in impotent rage.

When Phatik came into the house, his mother saw him. She called out angrily: "So you have been hitting Mākhan again?"

Phatik answered indignantly: "No, I haven't! Who told you that?"

His mother shouted: "Don't tell lies! You have."

Phatik said sullenly: "I tell you, I haven't. You ask Mākhan!" But Mākhan thought it best to stick to his previous statement. He said: "Yes, mother. Phatik did hit me."

Phatik's patience was already exhausted. He could not bear this injustice. He rushed at Mākhan and hammered him with blows: "Take that," he cried, "and that, and that, for telling lies."

His mother took Mākhan's side in a moment, and pulled Phatik away, beating him with her hands. When Phatik pushed her aside, she shouted out: "What! you little villain! Would you hit your own mother?"

It was just at this critical juncture that the grey-haired stranger arrived. He asked what was the matter. Phatik looked sheepish and ashamed.

But when his mother stepped back and looked at the stranger, her anger was changed to surprise. For she recognized her brother and cried: "Why, Dada! Where have you come from?"

As she said these words, she bowed to the ground and touched his feet. Her brother had gone away soon after she had married; and he had started business in Bombay. His sister had lost her husband while he was there. Bishamber had now come back to Calcutta and had at once made enquiries about his sister. He had then hastened to see her as soon as he found out where she was.

The next few days were full of rejoicing. The brother

asked after the education of the two boys. He was told by his sister that Phatik was a perpetual nuisance. He was lazy, disobedient, and wild. But Mākhan was as good as gold, as quiet as a lamb, and very fond of reading. Bishamber kindly offered to take Phatik off his sister's hands and educate him with his own children in Calcutta. The widowed mother readily agreed. When his uncle asked Phatik if he would like to go to Calcutta with him, his joy knew no bounds and he said: "Oh, yes, uncle!" in a way that made it quite clear that he meant it.

It was an immense relief to the mother to get rid of Phatik. She had a prejudice against the boy, and no love was lost between the two brothers. She was in daily fear that he would either drown Mākhan some day in the river, or break his head in a fight, or run him into some danger. At the same time she was a little distressed to see Phatik's extreme eagerness to get away.

Phatik, as soon as all was settled, kept asking his uncle every minute when they were to start. He was on pins and needles all day long with excitement and lay awake most of the night. He bequeathed to Mākhan, in perpetuity, his fishing-rod, his big kite, and his marbles. Indeed, at this time of departure, his generosity towards Mākhan was unbounded.

When they reached Calcutta, Phatik made the

acquaintance of his aunt for the first time. She was by no means pleased with this unnecessary addition to her family. She found her own three boys quite enough to manage without taking any one else. And to bring a village lad of fourteen into their midst was terribly upsetting. Bishamber should really have thought twice before committing such an indiscretion.

In this world of human affairs there is no worse nuisance than a boy at the age of fourteen. He is neither ornamental nor useful. It is impossible to shower affection on him as on a little boy; and he is always getting in the way. If he talks with a childish lisp he is called a baby, and if he answers in a grown-up way he is called impertinent. In fact any talk at all from him is resented. Then he is at the unattractive, growing age. He grows out of his clothes with indecent haste; his voice grows hoarse and breaks and quavers; his face grows suddenly angular and unsightly. It is easy to excuse the shortcomings of early childhood, but it is hard to tolerate even unavoidable lapses in a boy of fourteen. The lad himself becomes painfully self-conscious. When he talks with elderly people he is either unduly forward, or else so unduly shy that he appears ashamed of his very existence.

Yet it is at this very age when, in his heart of hearts, a young lad most craves for recognition and love; and he becomes the devoted slave of any one who shows him consideration. But none dare openly love him, for that would be regarded as undue indulgence and therefore bad for the boy. So, what with scolding and chiding, he becomes very much like a stray dog that has lost his master.

For a boy of fourteen his own home is the only Paradise. To live in a strange house with strange people is little short of torture, while the height of bliss is to receive the kind looks of women and never to be slighted by them.

It was anguish to Phatik to be the unwelcome guest in his aunt's house, despised by this elderly woman and slighted on every occasion. If ever she asked him to do anything for her, he would be so overjoyed that he would overdo it; and then she would tell him not to be so stupid, but to get on with his lessons.

The cramped atmosphere of neglect oppressed Phatik so much that he felt that he could hardly breathe. He wanted to go out into the open country and fill his lungs with fresh air. But there was no open country to go to. Surrounded on all sides by Calcutta houses and walls, he would dream night after night of his village home and long to be back there. He remembered the glorious meadow where he used to fly his kite all day long; the broad river-banks where he would wander about the live-long day singing and shouting for joy; the narrow brook where he could go and dive and swim at any time he liked. He thought of his band of boy companions over whom he was despot; and, above all, thememory of that tyrant mother of his, who had such a prejudice against him, occupied him day and night. A kind of physical love like that of animals, a longing to be in the presence of the one who is loved, an inexpressible wistfulness during absence, a silent cry of the inmost heart for the mother, like the lowing of a calf in the twilight,—this love, which was almost an animal instinct, agitated the shy, nervous, lean, uncouth and ugly boy. No one could understand it, but it preyed upon his mind continually.

There was no more backward boy in the whole school than Phatik. He gaped and remained silent when the teacher asked him a question, and like an overladen ass patiently suffered all the blows that came down on his back. When other boys were out at play, he stood wistfully by the window and gazed at the roofs of the distant houses. And if by chance he espied children playing on the open terrace of any roof, his heart would ache with longing.

One day he summoned up all his courage and asked his uncle: "Uncle, when can I go home?"

His uncle answered: "Wait till the holidays come."

But the holidays would not come till October and there was a long time still to wait.

One day Phatik lost his lesson book. Even with the help of books he had found it very difficult indeed to prepare his lesson. Now it was impossible. Day after day the teacher would cane him unmercifully. His condition became so abjectly miserable that even his cousins were ashamed to own him. They began to jeer and insult him more than the other boys. He went to his aunt at last and told her that he had lost his book.

His aunt pursed her lips in contempt and said: "You great clumsy, country lout! How can I afford, with all my family, to buy you new books five times a month?"

That night, on his way back from school, Phatik had a bad headache with a fit of shivering. He felt he was going to have an attack of malarial fever. His one great fear was that he would be a nuisance to his aunt.

The next morning Phatik was nowhere to be seen. All searches in the neighbourhood proved futile. The rain had been pouring in torrents all night, and those who went out in search of the boy got drenched through to the skin. At last Bishamber asked help from the police.

At the end of the day a police van stopped at the door before the house. It was still raining and the streets were all flooded. Two constables brought out Phatik in their arms and placed him before Bishamber. He was wet through from head to foot, muddy all over, his face and eyes flushed red with fever and his limbs trembling. Bishamber carried him in his arms and took him into the inner apartments. When his wife saw him she exclaimed: "What a heap of trouble this boy has given us! Hadn't you better send him home?"

Phatik heard her words and sobbed out loud: "Uncle, I was just going home; but they dragged me back again."

The fever rose very high, and all that night the boy was delirious. Bishamber brought in a doctor. Phatik opened his eyes, flushed with fever, and looked up to the ceiling and said vacantly: "Uncle, have the holidays come yet?"

Bishamber wiped the tears from his own eyes and took Phatik's lean and burning hands in his own and sat by him through the night. The boy began again to mutter. At last his voice became excited: "Mother!" he cried, "don't beat me like that Mother! I *am* telling the truth!"

The next day Phatik became conscious for a short time. He turned his eyes about the room, as if expecting some one to come. At last, with an air of disappointment, his head sank back on the pillow. He turned his face to the wall with a deep sigh.

Bishamber knew his thoughts and bending down his

head whispered: "Phatik, I have sent for your mother."

The day went by. The doctor said in a troubled voice that the boy's condition was very critical.

Phatik began to cry out: "By the mark—three fathoms. By the mark—four fathoms. By the mark——." He had heard the sailor on the river-steamer calling out the mark on the plumb-line. Now he was himself plumbing an unfathomable sea.

Later in the day Phatik's mother burst into the room, like a whirlwind, and began to toss from side to side and moan and cry in a loud voice.

Bishamber tried to calm her agitation, but she flung herself on the bed, and cried: "Phatik, my darling, my darling."

Phatik stopped his restless movements for a moment. His hands ceased beating up and down. He said: "Eh?"

The mother cried again: "Phatik, my darling, my darling."

Phatik very slowly turned his head and without seeing anybody said: "Mother, the holidays have come."

III

ONCE THERE WAS A KING

"Once upon a time there was a king."

When we were children there was no need to know who the king in the fairy story was. It didn't matter whether he was called Shiladitya or Shaliban, whether he lived at Kashi or Kanauj. The thing that made a seven-year-old boy's heart go thump, thump with delight was this one sovereign truth, this reality of all realities: "Once there was a king."

But the readers of this modern age are far more exact and exacting. When they hear such an opening to a story, they are at once critical and suspicious. They apply the searchlight of science to its legendary haze and ask: "Which king?"

The story-tellers have become more precise in their turn. They are no longer content with the old indefinite, "There was a king," but assume instead a look of profound learning and begin: "Once there was a king named Ajatasatru."

The modern reader's curiosity, however, is not so easily satisfied. He blinks at the author through his scientific spectacles and asks again: "Which Ajatasatru?"

When we were young, we understood all sweet things; and we could detect the sweets of a fairy story by an unerring science of our own. We never cared for such useless things as knowledge. We only cared for truth. And our unsophisticated little hearts knew well where the Crystal Palace of Truth lay and how to reach it. But to-day we are expected to write pages of facts, while the truth is simply this:

"There was a king."

I remember vividly that evening in Calcutta when the fairy story began. The rain and the storm had been incessant. The whole of the city was flooded. The water was knee-deep in our lane. I had a straining hope, which was almost a certainty, that my tutor would be prevented from coming that evening. I sat on the stool in the far corner of the verandah looking down the lane, with a heart beating faster and faster. Every minute I kept my eye on the rain, and when it began to diminish I prayed with all my might: "Please, God, send some more rain till half-past seven is over." For I was quite ready to believe that there was no other need for rain except to protect one helpless boy one evening in one corner of Calcutta from the deadly clutches of his tutor.

If not in answer to my prayer, at any rate according to some grosser law of nature, the rain did not give up.

But, alas, nor did my teacher!

Exactly to the minute, in the bend of the lane, I saw his approaching umbrella. The great bubble of hope burst in my breast, and my heart collapsed. Truly, if there is a punishment to fit the crime after death, then my tutor will be born again as me, and I shall be born as my tutor.

As soon as I saw his umbrella I ran as hard as I could to my mother's room. My mother and my grandmother were sitting opposite one another playing cards by the light of a lamp. I ran into the room, and flung myself on the bed beside my mother, and said:

"Mother, the tutor has come, and I have such a bad headache; couldn't I have no lessons to-day?"

I hope no child of immature age will be allowed to read this story, and I sincerely trust it will not be used in text-books or primers for junior classes. For what I did was dreadfully bad, and I received no punishment whatever. On the contrary, my wickedness was crowned with success.

My mother said to me: "All right," and turning to the servant added: "Tell the tutor that he can go back home."

It was perfectly plain that she didn't think my illness very serious, as she went on with her game as before and took no further notice. And I also, burying my head in the pillow, laughed to my heart's content. We perfectly understood one another, my mother and I.

But every one must know how hard it is for a boy of seven years old to keep up the illusion of illness for a long time. After about a minute I got hold of Grandmother and said: "Grannie, do tell me a story."

I had to ask this many times. Grannie and Mother went on playing cards and took no notice. At last Mother said to me: "Child, don't bother. Wait till we've finished our game." But I persisted: "Grannie, do tell me a story." I told Mother she could finish her game to-morrow, but she must let Grannie tell me a story there and then.

At last Mother threw down the cards and said: "You had better do what he wants. I can't manage him." Perhaps she had it in her mind that she would have no tiresome tutor on the morrow, while I should be obliged to be back at those stupid lessons.

As soon as ever Mother had given way, I rushed at

Grannie. I got hold of her hand, and, dancing with delight, dragged her inside my mosquito curtain on to the bed. I clutched hold of the bolster with both hands in my excitement, and jumped up and down with joy, and when I had got a little quieter said: "Now, Grannie, let's have the story!"

Grannie went on: "And the king had a queen."

That was good to begin with. He had only one!

It is usual for kings in fairy stories to be extravagant in queens. And whenever we hear that there are two queens our hearts begin to sink. One is sure to be unhappy. But in Grannie's story that danger was past. He had only one queen.

We next hear that the king had not got any son. At the age of seven I didn't think there was any need to bother if a man had no son. He might only have been in the way.

Nor are we greatly excited when we hear that the king has gone away into the forest to practise austerities in order to get a son. There was only one thing that would have made me go into the forest, and that was to get away from my tutor!

But the king left behind with his queen a small girl, who

grew up into a beautiful princess.

Twelve years pass away, and the king goes on practising austerities, and never thinks all this while of his beautiful daughter. The princess has reached the full bloom of her youth. The age of marriage has passed, but the king does not return. And the queen pines away with grief and cries: "Is my golden daughter destined to die unmarried? Ah me, what a fate is mine!"

Then the queen sent men to the king to entreat him earnestly to come back for a single night and take one meal in the palace. And the king consented.

The queen cooked with her own hand, and with the greatest care, sixty-four dishes. She made a seat for him of sandal-wood and arranged the food in plates of gold and cups of silver. The princess stood behind with the peacock-tail fan in her hand. The king, after twelve years' absence, came into the house, and the princess waved the fan, lighting up all the room with her beauty. The king looked in his daughter's face and forgot to take his food.

At last he asked his queen: "Pray, who is this girl whose beauty shines as the gold image of the goddess? Whose daughter is she?"

The queen beat her forehead and cried: "Ah, how evil is

my fate! Do you not know your own daughter?"

The king was struck with amazement. He said at last: "My tiny daughter has grown to be a woman."

"What else?" the queen said with a sigh. "Do you not know that twelve years have passed by?"

"But why did you not give her in marriage?" asked the king.

"You were away," the queen said. "And how could I find her a suitable husband?"

The king became vehement with excitement. "The first man I see to-morrow," he said, "when I come out of the palace shall marry her."

The princess went on waving her fan of peacock feathers, and the king finished his meal.

The next morning, as the king came out of his palace, he saw the son of a Brahman gathering sticks in the forest outside the palace gates. His age was about seven or eight.

The King said: "I will marry my daughter to him."

Who can interfere with a king's command? At once the boy was called, and the marriage garlands were exchanged between him and the princess.

At this point I came up close to my wise Grannie and asked her eagerly: "When then?"

In the bottom of my heart there was a devout wish to substitute myself for that fortunate wood-gatherer of seven years old. The night was resonant with the patter of rain. The earthen lamp by my bedside was burning low. My grandmother's voice droned on as she told the story. And all these things served to create in a corner of my credulous heart the belief that I had been gathering sticks in the dawn of some indefinite time in the kingdom of some unknown king, and in a moment garlands had been exchanged between me and the princess, beautiful as the Goddess of Grace. She had a gold band on her hair and gold earrings in her ears. She had a necklace and bracelets of gold, and a golden waist-chain round her waist, and a pair of golden anklets tinkled above her feet.

If my grandmother were an author, how many explanations she would have to offer for this little story! First of all, every one would ask why the king remained twelve years in the forest? Secondly, why should the king's daughter remain unmarried all that while? This would be regarded as absurd.

Even if she could have got so far without a quarrel,

still there would have been a great hue and cry about the marriage itself. First, it never happened. Secondly, how could there be a marriage between a princess of the Warrior Caste and a boy of the priestly Brahman Caste? Her readers would have imagined at once that the writer was preaching against our social customs in an underhand way. And they would write letters to the papers.

So I pray with all my heart that my grandmother may be born a grandmother again, and not through some cursed fate take birth as her luckless grandson.

With a throb of joy and delight, I asked Grannie: "What then?"

Grannie went on: Then the princess took her little husband away in great distress, and built a large palace with seven wings, and began to cherish her husband with great care.

I jumped up and down in my bed and clutched at the bolster more tightly than ever and said: "What then?"

Grannie continued: The little boy went to school and learnt many lessons from his teachers, and as he grew up his class-fellows began to ask him: "Who is that beautiful lady living with you in the palace with the seven wings?"

The Brahman's son was eager to know who she was. He could only remember how one day he had been gathering sticks and a great disturbance arose. But all that was so long ago that he had no clear recollection.

Four or five years passed in this way. His companions always asked him: "Who is that beautiful lady in the palace with the seven wings?" And the Brahman's son would come back from school and sadly tell the princess: "My school companions always ask me who is that beautiful lady in the palace with the seven wings, and I can give them no reply. Tell me, oh, tell me, who you are!"

The princess said: "Let it pass to-day. I will tell you some other day." And every day the Brahman's son would ask: "Who are you?" and the princess would reply: "Let it pass to-day. I will tell you some other day." In this manner four or five more years passed away.

At last the Brahman's son became very impatient and said: "If you do not tell me to-day who you are, O beautiful lady, I will leave this palace with the seven wings." Then the princess said: "I will certainly tell you to-morrow."

Next day the Brahman's son, as soon as he came home from school, said: "Now, tell me who you are." The princess said: "To-night I will tell you after supper, when you are in bed."

The Brahman's son said: "Very well"; and he began to count the hours in expectation of the night. And the princess, on her side, spread white flowers over the golden bed, and lighted a gold lamp with fragrant oil, and adorned her hair, and dressed herself in a beautiful robe of blue, and began to count the hours in expectation of the night.

That evening when her husband, the Brahman's son, had finished his meal, too excited almost to eat, and had gone to the golden bed in the bedchamber strewn with flowers, he said to himself: "To-night I shall surely know who this beautiful lady is in the palace with the seven wings."

The princess took for her food that which was left over by her husband, and slowly entered the bedchamber. She had to answer that night the question, who was the beautiful lady that lived in the palace with the seven wings. And as she went up to the bed to tell him she found a serpent had crept out of the flowers and had bitten the Brahman's son. Her boy-husband was lying on the bed of flowers, with face pale in death.

My heart suddenly ceased to throb, and I asked with choking voice: "What then?"

Grannie said: "Then ..."

But what is the use of going on any further with the

story? It would only lead on to what was more and more impossible. The boy of seven did not know that, if there were some "What then?" after death, no grandmother of a grandmother could tell us all about it.

But the child's faith never admits defeat, and it would snatch at the mantle of death itself to turn him back. It would be outrageous for him to think that such a story of one teacherless evening could so suddenly come to a stop. Therefore the grandmother had to call back her story from the ever-shut chamber of the great End, but she does it so simply: it is merely by floating the dead body on a banana stem on the river, and having some incantations read by a magician. But in that rainy night and in the dim light of a lamp death loses all its horror in the mind of the boy, and seems nothing more than a deep slumber of a single night. When the story ends the tired eyelids are weighed down with sleep. Thus it is that we send the little body of the child floating on the back of sleep over the still water of time, and then in the morning read a few verses of incantation to restore him to the world of life and light.

IV

THE CHILD'S RETURN

I

Raicharan was twelve years old when he came as a servant to his master's house. He belonged to the same caste as his master and was given his master's little son to nurse. As time went on the boy left Raicharan's arms to go to school. From school he went on to college, and after college he entered the judicial service. Always, until he married, Raicharan was his sole attendant.

But when a mistress came into the house, Raicharan found two masters instead of one. All his former influence passed to the new mistress. This was compensated by a fresh arrival. Anukul had a son born to him and Raicharan by his unsparing attentions soon got a complete hold over the child. He used to toss him up in his arms, call to him in absurd baby language, put his face close to the baby's and draw it away again with a laugh.

Presently the child was able to crawl and cross the doorway. When Raicharan went to catch him, he would scream with mischievous laughter and make for safety. Raicharan was amazed at the profound skill and exact judgment the baby showed when pursued. He would say to his mistress with a look of awe and mystery: "Your son will be a judge some day."

New wonders came in their turn. When the baby began to toddle, that was to Raicharan an epoch in human history. When he called his father Ba-ba and his mother Ma-ma and Raicharan Chan-na, then Raicharan's ecstasy knew no bounds. He went out to tell the news to all the world.

After a while Raicharan was asked to show his ingenuity in other ways. He had, for instance, to play the part of a horse, holding the reins between his teeth and prancing with his feet. He had also to wrestle with his little charge; and if he could not, by a wrestler's trick, fall on his back defeated at the end a great outcry was certain.

About this time Anukul was transferred to a district on the banks of the Padma. On his way through Calcutta he bought his son a little go-cart. He bought him also a yellow satin waistcoat, a gold-laced cap, and some gold bracelets and anklets. Raicharan was wont to take these out and put them on his little charge, with ceremonial pride, whenever they went for a walk.

Then came the rainy season and day after day the rain poured down in torrents. The hungry river, like an enormous serpent, swallowed down terraces, villages, cornfields, and covered with its flood the tall grasses and wild casuarinas on the sandbanks. From time to time there was a deep thud as the river-banks crumbled. The unceasing roar of the main current could be heard from far away. Masses of foam, carried swiftly past, proved to the eye the swiftness of the stream.

One afternoon the rain cleared. It was cloudy, but cool and bright. Raicharan's little despot did not want to stay in on such a fine afternoon. His lordship climbed into the go-cart. Raicharan, between the shafts, dragged him slowly along till he reached the rice-fields on the banks of the river. There was no one in the fields and no boat on the stream. Across the water, on the farther side, the clouds were rifted in the west. The silent ceremonial of the setting sun was revealed in all its glowing splendour. In the midst of that stillness the child, all of a sudden, pointed with his finger in front of him and cried: "Chan-na! Pitty fow."

Close by on a mud-flat stood a large *Kadamba* tree in full flower. My lord, the baby, looked at it with greedy eyes and Raicharan knew his meaning. Only a short time before he had made, out of these very flower balls, a small go-cart; and the child had been so entirely happy dragging it about with a string, that for the whole day Raicharan was not asked to put on the reins at all. He was promoted from a horse into a groom.

But Raicharan had no wish that evening to go splashing knee-deep through the mud to reach the flowers. So he quickly pointed his finger in the opposite direction, calling out: "Look, baby, look! Look at the bird." And with all sorts of curious noises he pushed the go-cart rapidly away from the tree.

But a child, destined to be a judge, cannot be put off so easily. And besides, there was at the time nothing to attract his eyes. And you cannot keep up for ever the pretence of an imaginary bird.

The little Master's mind was made up, and Raicharan was at his wits' end. "Very well, baby," he said at last, "you sit still in the cart, and I'll go and get you the pretty flower. Only mind you don't go near the water."

As he said this, he made his legs bare to the knee, and waded through the oozing mud towards the tree.

The moment Raicharan had gone, his little Master's thoughts went off at racing speed to the forbidden water. The baby saw the river rushing by, splashing and gurgling as it went. It seemed as though the disobedient wavelets themselves were running away from some greater Raicharan with the laughter of a thousand children. At the sight of their mischief, the heart of the human child grew excited and restless. He got down stealthily from the go-cart and toddled off towards the river. On his way he picked up a small stick and leant over the bank of the stream pretending to fish. The mischievous fairies of the river with their mysterious voices seemed inviting him into their play-house.

Raicharan had plucked a handful of flowers from the tree and was carrying them back in the end of his cloth, with his face wreathed in smiles. But when he reached the go-cart there was no one there. He looked on all sides and there was no one there. He looked back at the cart and there was no one there.

In that first terrible moment his blood froze within him. Before his eyes the whole universe swam round like a dark mist. From the depth of his broken heart he gave one piercing cry: "Master, Master, little Master."

But no voice answered "Chan-na." No child laughed mischievously back: no scream of baby delight welcomed his return. Only the river ran on with its splashing, gurgling noise as before,—as though it knew nothing at all and had no time to attend to such a tiny human event as the death of a child.

As the evening passed by Raicharan's mistress became very anxious. She sent men out on all sides to search. They went with lanterns in their hands and reached at last the banks of the Padma. There they found Raicharan rushing up and down the fields, like a stormy wind, shouting the cry of despair: "Master, Master, little Master!"

When they got Raicharan home at last, he fell prostrate at the feet of his mistress. They shook him, and questioned him, and asked him repeatedly where he had left the child; but all he could say was that he knew nothing.

Though every one held the opinion that the Padma had swallowed the child, there was a lurking doubt left in the mind. For a band of gipsies had been noticed outside the village that afternoon, and some suspicion rested on them. The mother went so far in her wild grief as to think it possible that Raicharan himself had stolen the child. She called him aside with piteous entreaty and said: "Raicharan, give me back my baby. Give me back my child. Take from me any money you ask, but give me back my child!"

Raicharan only beat his forehead in reply. His mistress ordered him out of the house.

Anukul tried to reason his wife out of this wholly unjust suspicion: "Why on earth," he said, "should he commit such a crime as that?"

The mother only replied: "The baby had gold ornaments on his body. Who knows?"

It was impossible to reason with her after that.

II

Raicharan went back to his own village. Up to this time he had had no son, and there was no hope that any child would now be born to him. But it came about before the end of a year that his wife gave birth to a son and died.

An overwhelming resentment at first grew up in Raicharan's heart at the sight of this new baby. At the back of his mind was resentful suspicion that it had come as a usurper in place of the little Master. He also thought it would be a grave offence to be happy with a son of his own after what had happened to his master's little child. Indeed, if it had not been for a widowed sister, who mothered the new baby, it would not have lived long.

But a change gradually came over Raicharan's mind. A wonderful thing happened. This new baby in turn began to crawl about, and cross the doorway with mischief in its face. It also showed an amusing cleverness in making its escape to safety. Its voice, its sounds of laughter and tears, its gestures, were those of the little Master. On some days, when Raicharan listened to its crying, his heart suddenly began thumping wildly against his ribs, and it seemed to him that his former little Master was crying somewhere in the unknown land of death because he had lost his Chan-na.

Phailna (for that was the name Raicharan's sister gave to the new baby) soon began to talk. It learnt to say Ba-ba and Ma-ma with a baby accent. When Raicharan heard those familiar sounds the mystery suddenly became clear. The little Master could not cast off the spell of his Chan-na and therefore he had been reborn in his own house.

The three arguments in favour of this were, to Raicharan, altogether beyond dispute:

The new baby was born soon after his little master's death.

His wife could never have accumulated such merit as to give birth to a son in middle age.

The new baby walked with a toddle and called out Ba-ba and Ma-ma.—There was no sign lacking which marked out the future judge.

Then suddenly Raicharan remembered that terrible accusation of the mother. "Ah," he said to himself with amazement, "the mother's heart was right. She knew I had stolen her child."

When once he had come to this conclusion, he was filled with remorse for his past neglect. He now gave himself over, body and soul, to the new baby and became its devoted attendant. He began to bring it up as if it were the son of a rich man. He bought a go-cart, a yellow satin waistcoat, and a gold-embroidered cap. He melted down the ornaments of his dead wife and made gold bangles and anklets. He refused to let the little child play with any one of the neighbourhood and became himself its sole companion day and night. As the baby grew up to boyhood, he was so petted and spoilt and clad in such finery that the village children would call him "Your Lordship," and jeer at him; and older people regarded Raicharan as unaccountably crazy about the child.

At last the time came for the boy to go to school. Raicharan sold his small piece of land and went to Calcutta. There he got employment with great difficulty as a servant and sent Phailna to school. He spared no pains to give him the best education, the best clothes, the best food. Meanwhile, he himself lived on a mere handful of rice and would say in secret: "Ah, my little Master, my dear little Master, you loved me so much that you came back to my house! You shall never suffer from any neglect of mine."

Twelve years passed away in this manner. The boy was able to read and write well. He was bright and healthy and good-looking. He paid a great deal of attention to his personal appearance and was specially careful in parting his hair. He was inclined to extravagance and finery and spent money freely. He could never quite look on Raicharan as a father, because, though fatherly in affection, he had the manner of a servant. A further fault was this, that Raicharan kept secret from every one that he himself was the father of the child.

The students of the hostel, where Phailna was a boarder, were greatly amused by Raicharan's country manners, and I have to confess that behind his father's back Phailna joined in their fun. But, in the bottom of their hearts, all the students loved the innocent and tender-hearted old man, and Phailna was very fond of him also. But, as I have said before, he loved him with a kind of condescension.

Raicharan grew older and older, and his employer was continually finding fault with him for his incompetent work. He had been starving himself for the boy's sake, so he had grown physically weak and no longer up to his daily task. He would forget things and his mind became dull and stupid. But his employer expected a full servant's work out of him and would not brook excuses. The money that Raicharan had brought with him from the sale of his land was exhausted. The boy was continually grumbling about his clothes and asking for more money.

III

Raicharan made up his mind. He gave up the situation where he was working as a servant, and left some money with Phailna and said: "I have some business to do at home in my village, and shall be back soon."

He went off at once to Baraset where Anukul was magistrate. Anukul's wife was still broken down with grief. She had had no other child.

One day Anukul was resting after a long and weary day in court. His wife was buying, at an exorbitant price, a herb from a mendicant quack, which was said to ensure the birth of a child. A voice of greeting was heard in the courtyard. Anukul went out to see who was there. It was Raicharan. Anukul's heart was softened when he saw his old servant. He asked him many questions and offered to take him back into service.

Raicharan smiled faintly and said in reply: "I want to make obeisance to my mistress."

Anukul went with Raicharan into the house, where the mistress did not receive him as warmly as his old master.

Raicharan took no notice of this, but folded his hands and said: "It was not the Padma that stole your baby. It was I."

Anukul exclaimed: "Great God! Eh! What! Where is he?"

Raicharan replied: "He is with me. I will bring him the day after to-morrow."

It was Sunday. There was no magistrate's court sitting. Both husband and wife were looking expectantly along the road, waiting from early morning for Raicharan's appearance. At ten o'clock he came leading Phailna by the hand.

Anukul's wife, without a question, took the boy into her lap and was wild with excitement, sometimes laughing, sometimes weeping, touching him, kissing his hair and his forehead, and gazing into his face with hungry, eager eyes. The boy was very good-looking and dressed like a gentleman's son. The heart of Anukul brimmed over with a sudden rush of affection.

Nevertheless the magistrate in him asked: "Have you any proofs?"

Raicharan said: "How could there be any proof of such a deed? God alone knows that I stole your boy, and no one else in the world."

When Anukul saw how eagerly his wife was clinging to the boy, he realised the futility of asking for proofs. It would be wiser to believe. And then,—where could an old man like Raicharan get such a boy from? And why should his faithful servant deceive him for nothing?

"But," he added severely, "Raicharan, you must not stay here."

"Where shall I go, Master?" said Raicharan, in a choking voice, folding his hands. "I am old. Who will take in an old man as a servant?"

The mistress said: "Let him stay. My child will be pleased. I forgive him."

But Anukul's magisterial conscience would not allow him. "No," he said, "he cannot be forgiven for what he has done."

Raicharan bowed to the ground and clasped Anukul's feet. "Master," he cried, "let me stay. It was not I who did it. It was God."

Anukul's conscience was more shocked than ever when Raicharan tried to put the blame on God's shoulders.

"No," he said, "I could not allow it. I cannot trust you any more. You have done an act of treachery."

Raicharan rose to his feet and said: "It was not I who did it."

"Who was it then?" asked Anukul.

Raicharan replied: "It was my fate."

But no educated man could take this for an excuse. Anukul remained obdurate.

When Phailna saw that he was the wealthy magistrate's son, and not Raicharan's, he was angry at first, thinking that he had been cheated all this time of his birthright. But seeing Raicharan in distress, he generously said to his father: "Father, forgive him. Even if you don't let him live with us, let him have a small monthly pension."

After hearing this, Raicharan did not utter another word. He looked for the last time on the face of his son. He made obeisance to his old master and mistress. Then he went out and was mingled with the numberless people of the world.

At the end of the month Anukul sent him some money to his village. But the money came back. There was no one there of the name of Raicharan.

V
MASTER MASHAI

I

Adhar Babu lives upon the interest of the capital left him by his father. Only the brokers, negotiating loans, come to his drawing room and smoke the silver-chased hookah, and the clerks from the attorney's office discuss the terms of some mortgage or the amount of the stamp fees. He is so careful with his money that even the most dogged efforts of the boys from the local football club fail to make any impression on his pocket.

At the time this story opens a new guest came into his household. After a long period of despair, his wife, Nanibala, bore him a son.

The child resembled his mother,—large eyes, well-formed nose, and fair complexion. Ratikanta, Adharlal's protégé, gave verdict,—"He is worthy of this noble house."

They named him Venugopal.

Never before had Adharlal's wife expressed any opinion differing from her husband's on household expenses. There had been a hot discussion now and then about the propriety of some necessary item and up to this time she had merely acknowledged defeat with silent contempt. But now Adharlal could no longer maintain his supremacy. He had to give way little by little when things for his son were in question.

II

As Venugopal grew up, his father gradually became accustomed to spending money on him. He obtained an old teacher, who had a considerable repute for his learning and also for his success in dragging impassable boys through their examinations. But such a training does not lead to the cultivation of amiability. This man tried his best to win the boy's heart, but the little that was left in him of the natural milk of human kindness had turned sour, and the child repulsed his advances from the very beginning. The mother, in consequence, objected to him strongly, and complained that the very sight of him made her boy ill. So the teacher left.

Just then, Haralal made his appearance with a dirty dress and a torn pair of old canvas shoes. Haralal's mother, who was a widow, had kept him with great difficulty at a District school out of the scanty earnings which she made by cooking in strange houses and husking rice. He managed to pass the Matriculation and determined to go to College. As a result of his half-starved condition, his pinched face tapered to a point in an unnatural manner,—like Cape Comorin in the map of India; and the only broad portion of it was his forehead, which resembled the ranges of the Himalayas.

The servant asked Haralal what he wanted, and he answered timidly that he wished to see the master.

The servant answered sharply: "You can't see him." Haralal was hesitating, at a loss what to do next, when Venugopal, who had finished his game in the garden, suddenly came to the door. The servant shouted at Haralal: "Get away." Quite unaccountably Venugopal grew excited and cried: "No, he shan't get away." And he dragged the stranger to his father.

Adharlal had just risen from his mid-day sleep and was sitting quietly on the upper verandah in his cane chair, rocking his legs. Ratikanta was enjoying his hookah, seated in a chair next to him. He asked Haralal how far he had got in his reading. The young man bent his head and answered that he had passed the Matriculation. Ratikanta looked stern and expressed surprise that he should be so backward for his age. Haralal kept silence. It was Ratikanta's special pleasure to torture his patron's dependants, whether actual or potential.

Suddenly it struck Adharlal that he would be able to employ this youth as a tutor for his son on next to nothing. He agreed, there and then, to take him at a salary of five rupees a month with board and lodging free.

III

This time the post of tutor remained occupied longer than before. From the very beginning of their acquaintance Haralal and his pupil became great friends. Never before did Haralal have such an opportunity of loving any young human creature. His mother had been so poor and dependent, that he had never had the privilege of playing with the children where she was employed at work. He had not hitherto suspected the hidden stores of love which lay all the while accumulating in his own heart.

Venu, also, was glad to find a companion in Haralal. He was the only boy in the house. His two younger sisters were looked down upon, as unworthy of being his playmates. So his new tutor became his only companion, patiently bearing the undivided weight of the tyranny of his child friend.

IV

Venu was now eleven. Haralal had passed his Intermediate, winning a scholarship. He was working hard for his B.A. degree. After College lectures were over, he would take Venu out into the public park and tell him stories about the heroes from Greek History and Victor Hugo's romances. The child used to get quite impatient to run to Haralal, after school hours, in spite of his mother's attempts to keep him by her side.

This displeased Nanibala. She thought that it was a deep-laid plot of Haralal's to captivate her boy, in order to prolong his own appointment. One day she talked to him from behind the purdah: "It is your duty to teach my son only for an hour or two in the morning and evening. But why are you always with him? The child has nearly forgotten his own parents. You must understand that a man of your position is no fit companion for a boy belonging to this house."

Haralal's voice choked a little as he answered that for the future he would merely be Venu's teacher and would keep away from him at other times.

It was Haralal's usual practice to begin his College study early before dawn. The child would come to him directly after he had washed himself. There was a small pool in the garden and they used to feed the fish in it with puffed rice. Venu was also engaged in building a miniature garden-house, at the corner of the garden, with its liliputian gates and hedges and gravel paths. When the sun became too hot they would go back into the house, and Venu would have his morning lesson from Haralal.

On the day in question Venu had risen earlier than usual, because he wished to hear the end of the story which Haralal had begun the evening before. But he found his teacher absent. When asked about him, the door-servant said that he had gone out. At lesson time Venu remained unnaturally quiet. He never even asked Haralal why he had gone out, but went on mechanically with his lessons.

When the child was with his mother taking his breakfast, she asked him what had happened to make him so gloomy, and why he was not eating his food. Venu gave no answer. After his meal his mother caressed him and questioned him repeatedly. Venu burst out crying and said,—"Master Mashai." His mother asked Venu,—"What about Master Mashai?" But Venu found it difficult to name the offence which his teacher had committed.

His mother said to Venu: "Has your Master Mashai been saying anything to you against *me*?"

Venu could not understand the question and went away.

V

There was a theft in Adhar Babu's house. The police were called in to investigate. Even Haralal's trunks were searched. Ratikanta said with meaning: "The man who steals anything, does not keep his thefts in his own box."

Adharlal called his son's tutor and said to him: "It will not be convenient for me to keep any of you in my own house. From to-day you will have to take up your quarters outside, only coming in to teach my son at the proper time."

Ratikanta said sagely, drawing at his hookah: "That is a good proposal,—good for both parties."

Haralal did not utter a word, but he sent a letter saying that it would be no longer possible for him to remain as tutor to Venu.

When Venu came back from school, he found his tutor's room empty. Even that broken steel trunk of his was absent. The rope was stretched across the corner, but there were no clothes or towel hanging on it. Only on the table, which formerly was strewn with books and papers, stood a bowl containing some gold-fish with a label on which was written the word "Venu" in Haralal's handwriting. The boy ran up at once to his father and asked him what had happened. His father told him that Haralal had resigned his post. Venu went to his room and flung himself down and began to cry. Adharlal did not know what to do with him.

The next day, when Haralal was sitting on his wooden bedstead in the Hostel, debating with himself whether he should attend his college lectures, suddenly he saw Adhar Babu's servant coming into his room followed by Venu. Venu at once ran up to him and threw his arms round his neck asking him to come back to the house.

Haralal could not explain why it was absolutely impossible for him to go back, but the memory of those clinging arms and that pathetic request used to choke his breath with emotion long after.

VI

Haralal found out, after this, that his mind was in an unsettled state, and that he had but a small chance of winning the scholarship, even if he could pass the examination. At the same time, he knew that, without the scholarship, he could not continue his studies. So he tried to get employment in some office.

Fortunately for him, an English Manager of a big merchant firm took a fancy to him at first sight. After only a brief exchange of words the Manager asked him if he had any experience, and could he bring any testimonial. Haralal could only answer "No"; nevertheless a post was offered him of twenty rupees a month and fifteen rupees were allowed him in advance to help him to come properly dressed to the office.

The Manager made Haralal work extremely hard. He had to stay on after office hours and sometimes go to his master's house late in the evening. But, in this way, he learnt his work quicker than others, and his fellow clerks became jealous of him and tried to injure him, but without effect. He rented a small house in a narrow lane and brought his mother to live with him as soon as his salary was raised to forty rupees a month. Thus happiness came back to his mother after weary years of waiting.

Haralal's mother used to express a desire to see Venugopal, of whom she had heard so much. She wished to prepare some dishes with her own hand and to ask him to come just once to dine with her son. Haralal avoided the subject by saying that his house was not big enough to invite him for that purpose.

VII

The news reached Haralal that Venu's mother had died. He could not wait a moment, but went at once to Adharlal's house to see Venu. After that they began to see each other frequently.

But times had changed. Venu, stroking his budding moustache, had grown quite a young man of fashion. Friends, befitting his present condition, were numerous. That old dilapidated study chair and ink-stained desk had vanished, and the room now seemed to be bursting with pride at its new acquisitions,—its looking-glasses, oleographs, and other furniture. Venu had entered college, but showed no haste in crossing the boundary of the Intermediate examination.

Haralal remembered his mother's request to invite Venu to dinner. After great hesitation, he did so. Venugopal, with his handsome face, at once won the mother's heart. But as soon as ever the meal was over he became impatient to go, and looking at his gold watch he explained that he had pressing engagements elsewhere. Then he jumped into his carriage, which was waiting at the door, and drove away. Haralal with a sigh said to himself that he would never invite him again.

VIII

One day, on returning from office, Haralal noticed the presence of a man in the dark room on the ground floor of his house. Possibly he would have passed him by, had not the heavy scent of some foreign perfume attracted his attention. Haralal asked who was there, and the answer came:

"It is I, Master Mashai."

"What is the matter, Venu?" said Haralal. "When did you arrive?"

"I came hours ago," said Venu. "I did not know that you returned so late."

They went upstairs together and Haralal lighted the lamp and asked Venu whether all was well. Venu replied that his college classes were becoming a fearful bore, and his father did not realize how dreadfully hard it was for him to go on in the same class, year after year, with students much younger than himself. Haralal asked him what he wished to do. Venu then told him that he wanted to go to England and become a barrister. He gave an instance of a student, much less advanced than himself, who was getting ready to go. Haralal asked him if he had received his father's permission. Venu replied that his father would not hear a word of it until he had passed the Intermediate, and that was an impossibility in his present frame of mind. Haralal suggested that he himself should go and try to talk over his father.

"No," said Venu, "I can never allow that!"

Haralal asked Venu to stay for dinner and while they were waiting he gently placed his hand on Venu's shoulder and said:

"Venu, you should not quarrel with your father, or leave home."

Venu jumped up angrily and said that if he was not welcome, he could go elsewhere. Haralal caught him by the hand and implored him not to go away without taking his food. But Venu snatched away his hand and was just leaving the room when Haralal's mother brought the food in on a tray. On seeing Venu about to leave she pressed him to remain and he did so with bad grace.

While he was eating the sound of a carriage stopping at the door was heard. First a servant entered the room with creaking shoes and then Adhar Babu himself. Venu's face became pale. The mother left the room as soon as she saw strangers enter. Adhar Babu called out to Haralal in a voice thick with anger:

"Ratikanta gave me full warning, but I could not believe that you had such devilish cunning hidden in you. So, you think you're going to live upon Venu? This is sheer kidnapping, and I shall prosecute you in the Police Court."

Venu silently followed his father and went out of the house.

IX

The firm to which Haralal belonged began to buy up large quantities of rice and dhal from the country districts. To pay for this, Haralal had to take the cash every Saturday morning by the early train and disburse it. There were special centres where the brokers and middlemen would come with their receipts and accounts for settlement. Some discussion had taken place in the office about Haralal being entrusted with this work, without any security, but the Manager undertook all the responsibility and said that a security was not needed. This special work used to go on from the middle of December to the middle of April. Haralal would get back from it very late at night.

One day, after his return, he was told by his mother that Venu had called and that she had persuaded him to take his dinner at their house. This happened more than once. The mother said that it was because Venu missed his own mother, and the tears came into her eyes as she spoke about it.

One day Venu waited for Haralal to return and had a long talk with him.

"Master Mashai!" he said. "Father has become so cantankerous of late that I cannot live with him any longer. And, besides, I know that he is getting ready to marry again. Ratikanta is seeking a suitable match, and they are always conspiring about it. There used to be a time when my father would get anxious, if I were absent from home even for a few hours. Now, if I am away for more than a week, he takes no notice,—indeed he is greatly relieved. If this marriage takes place, I feel that I cannot live in the house any longer. You must show me a way out of this. I want to become independent."

Haralal felt deeply pained, but he did not know how to help his former pupil. Venu said that he was determined to go to England and become a barrister. Somehow or other he must get the passage money out of his father: he could borrow it on a note of hand and his father would have to pay when the creditors filed a suit. With this borrowed money he would get away, and when he was in England his father was certain to remit his expenses.

"But who is there," Haralal asked, "who would advance you the money?"

"You!" said Venu.

"I!" exclaimed Haralal in amazement.

"Yes," said Venu, "I've seen the servant bringing heaps of money here in bags." "The servant and the money belong to someone else."

Haralal explained why the money came to his house at night, like birds to their nest, to be scattered next morning.

"But can't the Manager advance the sum?" Venu asked.

"He may do so," said Haralal, "if your father stands security."

The discussion ended at this point.

X

One Friday night a carriage and pair stopped before Haralal's lodging house. When Venu was announced Haralal was counting money in his bedroom, seated on the floor. Venu entered the room dressed in a strange manner. He had discarded his Bengali dress and was wearing a Parsee coat and trousers and had a cap on his head. Rings were prominent on almost all the fingers of both hands, and a thick gold chain was hanging round his neck: there was a gold-watch in his pocket, and diamond studs could be seen peeping from his shirt sleeves. Haralal at once asked him what was the matter and why he was wearing that dress.

"My father's marriage," said Venu, "comes off to-morrow. He tried hard to keep it from me, but I found it out. I asked him to allow me to go to our garden-house at Barrackpur for a few days, and he was only too glad to get rid of me so easily. I am going there, and I wish to God I had never to come back."

Haralal looked pointedly at the rings on his fingers. Venu explained that they had belonged to his mother. Haralal then asked him if he had already had his dinner. He answered, "Yes, haven't you had yours?"

"No," said Haralal, "I cannot leave this room until I have all the money safely locked up in this iron chest."

"Go and take your dinner," said Venu, "while I keep guard here: your mother will be waiting for you."

For a moment Haralal hesitated, and then he went out and had his dinner. In a short time he came back with his mother and the three of them sat among the bags of money talking together. When it was about midnight, Venu took out his watch and looked at it and jumped up saying that he would miss his train. Then he asked Haralal to keep all his rings and his watch and chain until he asked for them again. Haralal put them all together in a leather bag and laid it in the iron safe. Venu went out.

The canvas bags containing the currency notes had already been placed in the safe: only the loose coins remained to be counted over and put away with the rest.

<h1 style="text-align:center">XI</h1>

Haralal lay down on the floor of the same room, with the key under his pillow, and went to sleep. He dreamt that Venu's mother was loudly reproaching him from behind the curtain. Her words were indistinct, but rays of different colours from the jewels on her body kept piercing the curtain like needles and violently vibrating. Haralal struggled to call Venu, but his voice seemed to forsake him. At last, with a noise, the curtain fell down. Haralal started up from his sleep and found darkness piled up round about him. A sudden gust of wind had flung open the window and put out the light. Haralal's whole body was wet with perspiration. He relighted the lamp and saw, by the clock, that it was four in the morning. There was no time to sleep again; for he had to get ready to start.

After Haralal had washed his face and hands his mother called from her own room,—"Baba, why are you up so soon?"

It was the habit of Haralal to see his mother's face the first thing in the morning in order to bring a blessing upon the day. His mother said to him: "I was dreaming that you were going out to bring back a bride for yourself." Haralal went to his own bedroom and began to take out the bags containing the silver and the currency notes.

Suddenly his heart stopped beating. Three of the bags appeared to be empty. He knocked them against the iron safe, but this only proved his fear to be true. He opened them and shook them with all his might. Two letters from Venu dropped out from one of the bags. One was addressed to his father and one to Haralal.

Haralal tore open his own letter and began reading. The words seemed to run into one another. He trimmed the lamp, but felt as if he could not understand what he read. Yet the purport of the letter was clear. Venu had taken three thousand rupees, in currency notes, and had started for England. The steamer was to sail before day-break that very morning. The letter ended with the words: "I am explaining everything in a letter to my father. He will pay off the debt; and then, again, my mother's ornaments, which I have left in your care, will more than cover the amount I have taken."

Haralal locked up his room and hired a carriage and went with all haste to the jetty. But he did not know even the name of the steamer which Venu had taken. He ran the whole length of the wharves from Prinsep's Ghat to Metiaburuj.

He found that two steamers had started on their voyage to England early that morning. It was impossible for him to know which of them carried Venu, or how to reach him.

When Haralal got home, the sun was strong and the whole of Calcutta was awake. Everything before his eyes seemed blurred. He felt as if he were pushing against a fearful obstacle which was bodiless and without pity. His mother came on the verandah to ask him anxiously where he had gone. With a dry laugh he said to her,—"To bring home a bride for myself," and then he fainted away.

On opening his eyes after a while, Haralal asked his mother to leave him. Entering his room he shut the door from the inside while his mother remained seated on the floor of the verandah in the fierce glare of the sun. She kept calling to him fitfully, almost mechanically,—"Baba, Baba!"

The servant came from the Manager's office and knocked at the door, saying that they would miss the train if they did not start out at once. Haralal called from inside, "It will not be possible for me to start this morning."

"Then where are we to go,

Sir?" "I will tell you later on."

The servant went downstairs with a gesture of

impatience.

Suddenly Haralal thought of the ornaments which Venu had left behind. Up till now he had completely forgotten about them, but with the thought came instant relief. He took the leather bag containing them, and also Venu's letter to his father, and left the house.

Before he reached Adharlal's house he could hear the bands playing for the wedding, yet on entering he could feel that there had been some disturbance. Haralal was told that there had been a theft the night before and one or two servants were suspected. Adhar Babu was sitting in the upper verandah flushed with anger and Ratikanta was smoking his hookah. Haralal said to Adhar Babu, "I have something private to tell you." Adharlal flared up, "I have no time now!" He was afraid that Haralal had come to borrow money or to ask his help. Ratikanta suggested that if there was any delicacy in making the request in his presence he would leave the place. Adharlal told him angrily to sit where he was. Then Haralal handed over the bag which Venu had left behind. Adharlal asked what was inside it and Haralal opened it and gave the contents into his hands.

Then Adhar Babu said with a sneer: "It's a paying business that you two have started—you and your former pupil! You were certain that the stolen property would be traced, and so you come along with it to me to claim a reward!"

Haralal presented the letter which Venu had written to his father. This only made Adharlal all the more furious.

"What's all this?" he shouted, "I'll call for the police! My son has not yet come of age,—and *you* have smuggled him out of the country! I'll bet my soul you've lent him a few hundred rupees, and then taken a note of hand for three thousand! But I am not going to be bound by *this*!"

"I never advanced him any money at all," said Haralal.

"Then how did he find it?" said Adharlal, "Do you mean to tell me he broke open your safe and stole it?"

Haralal stood silent.

Ratikanta sarcastically remarked: "I don't believe this fellow ever set hands on as much as three thousand rupees in his life."

When Haralal left the house he seemed to have lost the power of dreading anything, or even of being anxious. His mind seemed to refuse to work. Directly he entered the lane he saw a carriage waiting before his own lodging. For a moment he felt certain that it was Venu's. It was impossible to believe that his calamity could be so hopelessly final.

Haralal went up quickly, but found an English assistant from the firm sitting inside the carriage. The man came out when he saw Haralal and took him by the hand and asked him: "Why didn't you go out by train this morning?" The servant had told the Manager his suspicions and he had sent this man to find out.

Haralal answered: "Notes to the amount of three thousand rupees are missing." The man asked how that could have happened.

Haralal remained silent.

The man said to Haralal: "Let us go upstairs together and see where you keep your money." They went up to the room and counted the money and made a thorough search of the house.

When the mother saw this she could not contain herself any longer. She came out before the stranger and said: "Baba, what has happened?" He answered in broken Hindustani that some money had been stolen.

"Stolen!" the mother cried, "Why! How could it be stolen? Who could do such a dastardly thing?" Haralal said to her: "Mother, don't say a word."

The man collected the remainder of the money and told Haralal to come with him to the Manager. The mother barred the way and said:

"Sir, where are you taking my son? I have brought him up, starving and straining to do honest work. My son would never touch money belonging to others."

The Englishman, not knowing Bengali, said, "Achcha! Achcha!" Haralal told his mother not to be anxious; he would explain it all to the Manager and soon be back again. The mother entreated him, with a distressed voice,

"Baba, you haven't taken a morsel of food all morning." Haralal stepped into the carriage and drove away, and the mother sank to the ground in the anguish of her heart.

The Manager said to Haralal: "Tell me the truth. What did happen?"

Haralal said to him, "I haven't taken any money."

"I fully believe it," said the Manager, "but surely you know who has taken it."

Haralal looked on the ground and remained silent.

"Somebody," said the Manager, "must have taken it away with your connivance."

"Nobody," replied Haralal, "could take it away with my knowledge without taking first my life."

"Look here, Haralal," said the Manager, "I trusted you completely. I took no security. I employed you in a post of great responsibility. Every one in the office was against me for doing so. The three thousand rupees is a small matter, but the shame of all this to me is a great matter. I will do one thing. I will give you the whole day to bring back this money. If you do so, I shall say nothing about it and I will keep you on in your post."

It was now eleven o'clock. Haralal with bent head went out of the office. The clerks began to discuss the affair with exultation.

"What can I *do*? What can I *do*?" Haralal repeated to himself, as he walked along like one dazed, the sun's heat pouring down upon him. At last his mind ceased to think at all about what could be done, but the mechanical walk went on without ceasing.

This city of Calcutta, which offered its shelter to thousands and thousands of men had become like a steel trap. He could see no way out. The whole body of people were conspiring to surround and hold him captive—this most insignificant of men, whom no one knew. Nobody had any special grudge against him, yet everybody was his enemy. The crowd passed by, brushing against him: the clerks of the offices were eating their lunch on the road side from their plates made of leaves: a tired wayfarer on the Maidan, under the shade of a tree, was lying with one hand beneath his head and one leg upraised over the other: The up-country women, crowded into hackney carriages, were wending their way to the temple: a chuprassie came up with a letter and asked him the address on the envelope,— so the afternoon went by.

Then came the time when the offices were all about to close. Carriages started off in all directions, carrying people back to their homes. The clerks, packed tightly on the seats of the trams, looked at the theatre advertisements as they returned to their lodgings. From to-day, Haralal had neither his work in the office, nor release from work in the evening. He had no need to hurry to catch the tram to take him to his home. All the busy occupations of the city— the buildings—the horses and carriages—the incessant traffic—seemed, now at one time, to swell into dreadful reality, and at another time, to subside into the shadowy unreal.

Haralal had taken neither food, nor rest, nor shelter all that day.

The street lamps were lighted from one road to another

and it seemed to him that a watchful darkness, like some demon, was keeping its eyes wide open to guard every movement of its victim. Haralal did not even have the energy to enquire how late it was. The veins on his forehead throbbed, and he felt as if his head would burst. Through the paroxysms of pain, which alternated with the apathy of dejection, only one thought came again and again to his mind; among the innumerable multitudes in that vast city, only one name found its way through his dry throat,— "Mother!"

He said to himself, "At the deep of night, when no one is awake to capture me— me, who am the least of all men,—I will silently creep to my mother's arms and fall asleep, and may I never wake again!"

Haralal's one trouble was lest some police officer should molest him in the presence of his mother, and this kept him back from going home. When it became impossible for him at last to bear the weight of his own body, he hailed a carriage. The driver asked him where he wanted to go. He said: "Nowhere, I want to drive across the Maidan to get the fresh air." The man at first did not believe him and was about to drive on, when Haralal put a rupee into his hand as an advance payment. Thereupon the driver crossed, and then re-crossed, the Maidan from one side to the other, traversing the different roads.

Haralal laid his throbbing head on the side of the open window of the carriage and closed his eyes. Slowly all the pain abated. His body became cool. A deep and intense peace filled his heart and a supreme deliverance seemed to embrace him on every side. It was *not* true,—the day's despair which threatened him with its grip of utter helplessness. It was *not* true, it was false. He knew now that it was only an empty fear of the mind. Deliverance was in the infinite sky and there was no end to peace. No king or emperor in the world had the power to keep captive this nonentity, this Haralal. In the sky, surrounding his emancipated heart on every side, he felt the presence of his mother, that one poor woman. She seemed to grow and grow till she filled the infinity of darkness. All the roads and buildings and shops of Calcutta gradually became enveloped by her. In her presence vanished all the aching pains and thoughts and consciousness of Haralal. It burst,—that bubble filled with the hot vapour of pain. And now there was neither darkness nor light, but only one tense fulness.

The Cathedral clock struck one. The driver called out impatiently: "Babu, my horse can't go on any longer. Where do you want to go?"

There came no answer.

The driver came down and shook Haralal and asked him again where he wanted to go.

There came no answer.

And the answer was never received from Haralal, where he wanted to go.

NOTES

I. — THE KABULIWALAH

"The Kabuliwalah" is one of the most famous of the Poet's "Short Stories." It has been often translated. The present translation is by the late Sister Nivedita, and her simple, vivid style should be noticed by the Indian student reader. It is a good example of modern English, with its short sentences, its careful choice of words, and its luminous clearness of meaning.

Kabuliwalah.] A man from Cabul or Kabul, the capital of Afghanistan.

embarked.] Like a ship putting out to sea on a new voyage.

Bhola.] Mini's attendant.

Protap Singh.] Rabindranath Tagore pictures himself as engaged in writing a novel, full of wild adventures. These names are made up to suit the story.

so precarious.] The writer amusingly imagines the hero and heroine actually swinging by the rope until he can get back to his desk and finish writing about how they escaped.

Abdurrahman.] The Amir of Kabul.

Frontier policy.] The question about guarding the North-West of India against invasion.

without demur.] Without making any objection, or asking for more money.

judicious bribery.] He gave her little presents, *judging* well what she would like best.

new fangled.] The parents had not talked about such things, as old-fashioned people would have certainly done.

euphemism.] This means, in Greek, "fair speech." Here it means a pleasant word used instead of the unpleasant word "jail."

kings went forth.] During the hot weather the kings of ancient India used to stay at home: they would begin to fight again at the beginning of the cold weather.

my heart would go out.] That is to say, he would long to see such places.

fall to weaving.] This is an English idiom, like "set to": it means to begin.

conjure themselves.] Just as the conjurer makes all kinds of things appear before the eyes.

vegetable existence.] Vegetables are rooted to the ground. So Rabindranath is rooted to his desk and cannot make long journeys.

As it was indefinite.] Because there was no actual reason for it. Indefinite here means vague.

forbid the man the house.] This is a brief way of saying forbid the man to enter the house.

bebagged.] This word is made up for the occasion, and means "laden with bags." Compare the words bedewed, besmeared.

just where.] The word "just" has become very commonly used in modern English. It means "exactly," "merely" or "at the very moment." Compare "He had just gone out." "It was just a joke."

Scarcely on speaking terms.] Rabindranath Tagore is here making a joke; "not to be on speaking terms" means usually "to be displeased with." Mini had become so eager to talk with her girl friends that she had almost neglected her father.

Durga.] The Durga Festival in Bengal is supposed to represent the time when Parvati, or Durga, left her father's home in the Himalayas, called Kailas, and went to live with her husband, Siva.

Bhairavi.] One of the musical tunes which denotes separation.

chandeliers.] The glass ornamental hangings on which candles were lighted in great houses at weddings.

better-omened.] It was not considered a good omen, or good fortune, to meet a criminal on a wedding day.

dispersed.] Used up.

Parbati.] Another allusion to the Goddess Durga and her home in the Himalayas.

apparition.] This word comes from the same root as the word to "appear." It means a sudden or strange sight. It often means a ghost. Mini had so changed that when she appeared in her wedding dress she startled him, as if he had seen a ghost.

make friends with her anew.] His own daughter would

not know him at first.

Saw before him the barren mountains.] His memory was so strong that it made him forget the crowded Calcutta street and think of his home in the mountains.

II. — THE HOME-COMING

every one seconded the proposal.] All were so eagerly in favour that they wanted to speak at once in support of it.

regal dignity.] His position as a king of the other boys.

fertile brain.] Full of inventions and plans.

manoeuvre.] A French word meaning a plan of battle.

point of honour.] He would feel himself disgraced if he gave way.

Mother Earth.] Earth is here pictured as a person. There is a well-known story of a giant who gained fresh power every time his body touched the earth, which was his Mother.

Furies.] These were supposed to be certain demons, who pursued guilty men with loud cries.

the servant was master.] Notice the play of words here.

The "servant" and "master" change places.

critical juncture.] At this exact moment when things were so dangerous.

Dada.] The usual Bengal word for "Brother."

no love was lost.] This is a mild way of saying that they disliked one another.

on pins and needles.] Exceedingly restless; like some one standing on sharp points.

in perpetuity.] The phrase is a mock legal one, meaning "for all time."

by no means pleased.] She was very displeased, because she had already children of her own. In English a phrase is often put in a negative way to imply a very strong positive statement. Thus "by no means happy" may mean "very unhappy."

committing such an indiscretion.] Doing such an unwise thing.

indecent haste.] A mock humorous expression, meaning "very quickly."

craves for recognition.] Wishes to be noticed and loved.

physical love.] Just as a young animal clings to its mother for protection.

animal instinct.] The phrase repeats in another form what was said before, in the words "a kind of physical love."

pursed her lips.] Drew her lips tight like the mouth of a purse which is tightened by pulling the string.

as if expecting some one.] He was looking for his mother.

very critical.] Very dangerous. The danger point of the illness might be reached at any moment and death might come.

By the mark.] When a shallow place comes at sea, or on a great river, one of the sailors throws a piece of lead, with a string tied to it, into the water, and then looks at the *mark* on the string. He calls out that the depth is "three" or "four" fathoms according to the mark.

plumb-line.] The line with a lead weight.

plumbing.] To plumb is to get to the bottom of a piece of water. Here Phatik is pictured as himself going deeper and deeper into the sea of death, which none can fathom.

the holidays.] The Bengali word for "holiday" means

also "release." It is as though he were saying, "My release has come." This cannot be represented in the English.

III. — ONCE THERE WAS A KING

In this story Rabindranath Tagore begins with some amusing sentences about the dull, matter of fact character of modern scientific people, who cannot enjoy a fairy story without asking "Is it true?" The Poet implies that there are deeper truths than modern science has yet discovered. The ending of the present story will show this more clearly.

sovereign truth.] There is a play upon the word "sovereign" which can mean "kingly" and also "supreme."

exacting.] There is further play here with the words "exact" and "exacting." "Exact" means precise and "exacting" means making others precise.

legendary haze.] The ancient legends are very obscure, just like an object seen through a mist.

knowledge.] Mere book knowledge,—knowledge of outside things.

truth.] Inner truth such as comes from the heart of man and cannot be reasoned or disputed.

half past seven.] The time when his tutor was due.

no other need.] As if God would continue the rain merely to keep his tutor away!

If not.] Though it might not have been caused by his prayers, still for some reason the rain did continue.

nor did my teacher.] Supply the words "give up."

punishment to fit the crime.] An amusing reference to the doctrine of *karma*, which states that each deed will have its due reward or punishment.

as me.] Strictly speaking it should be "I" not "me" but he is writing not too strictly.

I hope no child.] The author here amusingly pretends that the child's way of getting out of his lessons was too shocking for young boys in the junior school to read about.

I will marry my daughter to him.] The verb to "marry" in English can be used

in two senses:—

(1) To wed some one: to take in marriage.

(2) To get some one wedded: to give in marriage. The later sense is used here.

in the dawn of some indefinite time.] In some past existence long ago.

If my grandmother were an author.] Here Rabindranath returns to his mocking humour. A modern author, he says, would be obliged to explain all sorts of details in the story.

hue and cry.] This is a phrase used for the noise and bustle that is made when people are searching for a thief.

Her readers.] Referring back to the Grandmother.

in an underhand way.] Under the disguise of a fairy story.

grandmother again.] That is, in the old conditions when people were not too exacting about accuracy.

luckless grandson.] A humorous way of referring to himself. The author had the misfortune to be born in the modern age of science.

Seven wings.] The word "wings" is here used, not for "wings" like those of birds, but for the sides of a large building, projecting out at an angle from the main building.

But what is the use....] The author here breaks off the story, as though it were useless to go on any further in these modern days when every thing has to be scientifically proved.

Some "what then?"] Some future existence about which explanations might be asked.

no grandmother of a grandmother.] No one, however old.

never admits defeat.] Refuses to believe in death.

teacherless evening.] Evening on which the teacher did not come.

chamber of the great end.] Death itself is referred to; it is the end of human life on earth and what is beyond death is shut out from us.

incantation.] Sacred verses or *mantras*.

IV. — THE RETURN OF THE CHILD

found two masters.] The wife was his master now, as well as her husband.

make for safety.] Get to some place where he could not be caught.

will be a judge some day.] The baby seemed so wise to Raicharan, that he thought he would certainly grow up to be a judge.

epoch in human history.] It seemed to Raicharan as though some great event had happened which ought to be recorded.

wrestler's trick.] The writer, in fun, makes Raicharan's skill depend on doing just what the wrestler tries to avoid, i.e. being thrown on his back.

swallowed down.] Washed them away in a flood.

little despot.] The baby, who was able to make Raicharan do exactly what he liked.

The silent ceremonial.] The author pictures the sunset as like some splendid kingly ceremony, where every gorgeous colour can be seen.

"Pitty fow."] "Pretty flower." The baby can only lisp the words.

He was promoted from a horse into a groom.] He was no longer asked by the baby to be a "horse" in his games, but to look after this toy carriage, as a groom would.

with all sorts of curious noises.] He began to imitate the sounds of birds.

destined to be a judge.] The baby could see through Raicharan's attempts to deceive, as a judge would see through false evidence.

wavelets.] The little waves seemed like so many thousand little children running away in fun or mischief.

there was no one there.] These words are repeated again and again to give the sense of utter loss and desolation.

overwhelming resentment.] His own baby seemed to have been given to him in order to tempt him to forget his little Master. Raicharan was angry to think that any one could imagine such forgetfulness to be possible.

The little Master could not cast off the spell.] Could not keep away from the servant who loved him so much. He fancies his little Master has come back to life again in this new little baby, drawn as it were by some enchantment of love.

accumulated.] Gathered together: referring to the idea of *karma*.

personal appearance.] He spent a long time in arranging his clothes and making himself look handsome.

country manners.] Country people have habits and

ways of speaking which seem absurd to town people.

a kind of condescension.] As if he were superior and Raicharan were beneath him.

mendicant quack.] A beggar dealing in herbs and medicines and charms.

hungry, eager eyes.] As if she could never gaze long enough upon him.

the magistrate in him.] The magistrate's way of looking at things.

magisterial conscience.] His instincts as a judge, who must condemn the guilty.

V. — MASTER MASHAI

Ratikanta.] He is represented throughout as a typical hanger-on of the rich family, selfish and flattering.

Victor Hugo.] The most famous of Victor Hugo's stories is called "Les Miserables." Its opening scene of San Valjean and the saintly Bishop is very well known in literature.

deep-laid plot.] Notice how throughout this story the different members of this wealthy house appear to be unable to take account of unselfish motives.

this is sheer kidnapping.] Adhar Babu believes that Haralal has acquired some hypnotic influence over Venu and is trying to rob him of his money.

brokers and middlemen.] Those who bought the grain from the peasants and sold it to the English firm.

any security.] A money payment which would be forfeited if anything went wrong.

a note of hand.] A paper signed by Venugopal saying that he owed so much money.

filed a suit.] Brought an action in the law courts against the father to recover the money lent to the son.

Currency notes.] Notes of twenty, fifty, a hundred rupees,—such as could be changed for money.

theft the night before.] Adhar Babu had already missed the things that Venu had taken away.

it's a paying business.] Adhar Babu imagines that Venu and Haralal have become partners in order to swindle other people.

with your connivance.] With your secret knowledge and approval.

Deliverance was in the infinite sky.] He felt that all the evils, which were pressing close around him, were broken through and that he had come out beyond them into the clear light of truth. It was like coming out of some narrow confined place into the open sky.